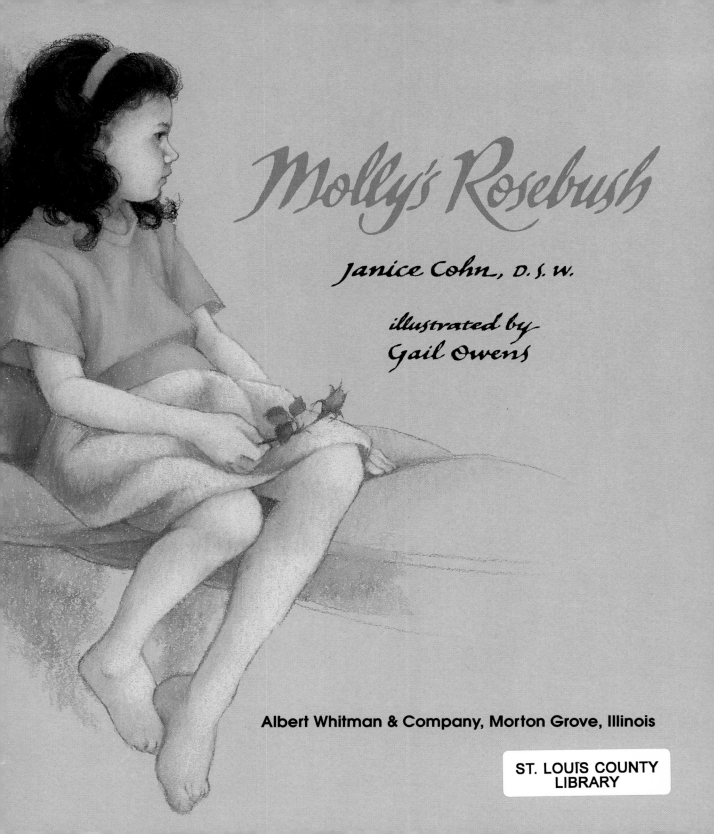

Molly's Rosebush

Janice Cohn, D. S. W.

illustrated by
Gail Owens

Albert Whitman & Company, Morton Grove, Illinois

Introduction for Parents

A miscarriage is a special kind of loss. With it comes the death of the many hopes, expectations, and plans surrounding the birth of a child. When a miscarriage occurs, there are usually no rituals or religious observances to help people heal. Yet there has been a genuine loss which affects both children and adults. How can young children be helped to understand and cope with a miscarriage? Here are some guidelines.

How are young children affected by a miscarriage?

Young children, characteristically, will center on how this event affects *them* and their world. They must deal with the fact that a new little sister or brother is not coming into the family, and that this means many events the family has planned will now not happen. They are often aware that Mommy and Daddy are feeling sad, upset, or preoccupied. They may have trouble understanding *why* the baby will not be born.

Exactly how each child is affected depends upon many things including his or her past history and personality, and the circumstances surrounding the miscarriage.

How should a miscarriage be explained to young children?

Explain the miscarriage as simply and directly as possible. You might tell the child that sometimes a baby isn't strong enough to survive in its mother's womb, and that this is what has happened to the baby you were expecting.

If your child asks *why* the baby wasn't strong enough, you may find an answer through your religious beliefs, or you may simply have to answer that no one really knows. Acknowledge that it can be hard not to have answers to things that are important to us.

Emphasize that not every unborn baby gets to be born, and that this is true with all living things. That's why when a baby *is* born, it's such a special and wonderful event.

Make sure your child understands that after a miscarriage, the baby will not be born and that it is no longer in its mother's womb. Sometimes children want to know where the baby is. This can be a difficult question to answer, especially in cases of a first or second trimester miscarriage. Again, often parents' responses can be guided by their religious or philosophical beliefs.

When a miscarriage occurs, it's often a difficult time for the family. Children can sense this, so don't try to hide your feelings. Instead, validate children's perceptions. Let them know that you're feeling sad or upset and emphasize that it takes some time for people to heal.

It's always appropriate to ask children how *they* are feeling. Some children will want to talk about their feelings, and others will not—or cannot—communicate their emotions. If that's the case, never pressure them to do so. Simply tell children that when and if they *do* feel like talking, you'll be there to listen. Then wait to see what questions children ask. Always take your cues from children themselves regarding how much information they want and need to hear, for every child has his or her own unique needs.

What kind of reactions are "normal" for children when they learn about a miscarriage?

Children may feel sad, confused, or disappointed, or they may not react intensely at all. Much will depend upon the point in the pregnancy at which the miscarriage occurred, the degree to which the child was involved with the plans for the new baby, and how aware the child is about how a fetus grows. Some children may have had mixed feelings about the coming baby and may even feel a little relieved.

Here, once again, it is best to take your cues directly from the child. Some children will need to be reassured that Mommy will be okay, especially if they are aware that their mother went to the hospital. Others will experience intense disappointment when they learn that they are not going to be a big brother or sister, and this issue will have to be addressed. Still other children will not be deeply affected by the miscarriage and will have neither the need nor the inclination to talk very much about it.

Many young children may not be able to express their emotions in words, so their *actions* will reflect how they are feeling. Some children will show they are upset by being very provocative and oppositional. If this occurs, keep in mind that children need clear limits regarding what is acceptable behavior, even when they are hurting.

Other children may become noticeably withdrawn. Still others may act out their version of a miscarriage in their play, and perhaps reenact it many times in an effort to work through their feelings. And there are children who may experience sleep or eating problems. None of these reactions should be cause for concern if they do not last longer than a week or two.

It's important to remember, however, that young children really do believe in magic; they are convinced that their thoughts and wishes can cause things to happen. Therefore, if at some point a child had wished that there wouldn't be a new baby, he or she might feel responsible when a miscarriage occurs. Keep this possibility in mind if a child seems to be having a particularly strong reaction.

When should a professional consultation be considered?

Sometimes an event such as a miscarriage triggers emotions that are associated with earlier, unresolved losses a child may have experienced. When this occurs, the child often evidences a noticeable behavior change or regresses to earlier, problematic behaviors (bed wetting, thumb sucking, sleep difficulties, etc.), which may persist for weeks or longer. If this is the case, a professional consultation can be helpful. Information about such consultations can be obtained from your child's pediatrician, a mental health center, or the pediatric psychiatry department of a medical center.

Janice Cohn

It was early summer, and Molly was snuggled in the window seat in her bedroom. An afternoon rain had just stopped falling, and sunshine had begun to filter through the light gray sky.

Molly was looking at the rosebush in the garden. Its pink petals glistened with raindrops, and it gave off a lovely, sweet fragrance that drifted in through the open window. The rosebush was very special to Molly and her mom and dad. And Molly was remembering why.

She thought about a day several months before.
It had been winter then, and very bright and cold.
Molly had had a busy day at school and was bursting
with things to tell Susan, her babysitter. But when
the school bus pulled up in front of her house, she
was surprised to see her dad waiting for her. He told
her that her mom was home resting, and that they
both wanted to talk with Molly.

When Molly and her dad went upstairs, they found
Molly's mother in bed, propped up with pillows. She
looked a little pale and tired. When Molly gave her a
hello kiss, she saw tears in her mom's eyes.

"Are you feeling sad, Mommy?" Molly asked,
touching her mom's cheek.

"Yes, honey, I am. Come cuddle beside me.
Daddy and I have something to tell you."

"It's about the new baby we've all been looking forward to," her dad said.

"Our new baby?" Molly asked.

Her dad nodded and took Molly's hand. "Mom and I found out today that our baby isn't going to be born."

"Ever?" asked Molly.

"Ever," said her dad.

"Remember the times we talked about how a baby grows inside its mommy's womb?" Molly's mom said. "Well, sometimes something happens, and the baby can't grow anymore. It's sort of like when a flower bud doesn't get to blossom into a flower. Even when a mommy takes very good care of the baby inside her, sometimes it's just not strong enough to live."

"But . . . why did it happen? Why did it happen to *our* baby?"

"We don't really know, Molly," her dad told her. "Some people think that God decides these things, for reasons we don't understand. Some people think it's just the way things happen in nature."

Molly was quiet for a bit. And then her mom asked gently, "Do you want to tell us what you're thinking?"

"Well . . . is our baby still inside you?"

"That's a very good question," her mom said. "The baby isn't in my womb any- more. After a baby stops growing, it leaves the mommy's body. Sometimes this happens by itself, and sometimes the doctor helps."

"Did you have to go to the doctor?"

"Yes, I did," her mom told her.

"Are you feeling sick?" asked Molly, a little worried.

"I'm just tired," her mom said. "So I'm going to get lots of rest for the next couple of days, and then I'll be fine."

That made Molly feel better, and she lay quietly in her mother's arms.

After a little while, her dad told Molly that it was time for her mom to take a nap. As he and Molly headed downstairs, Molly asked, "Will we *ever* have a new baby?"

"Well, I'm not sure, honey. I hope so," said her dad. "But no matter what happens, do you know what the most important thing is? That we have each other to love and to care for."

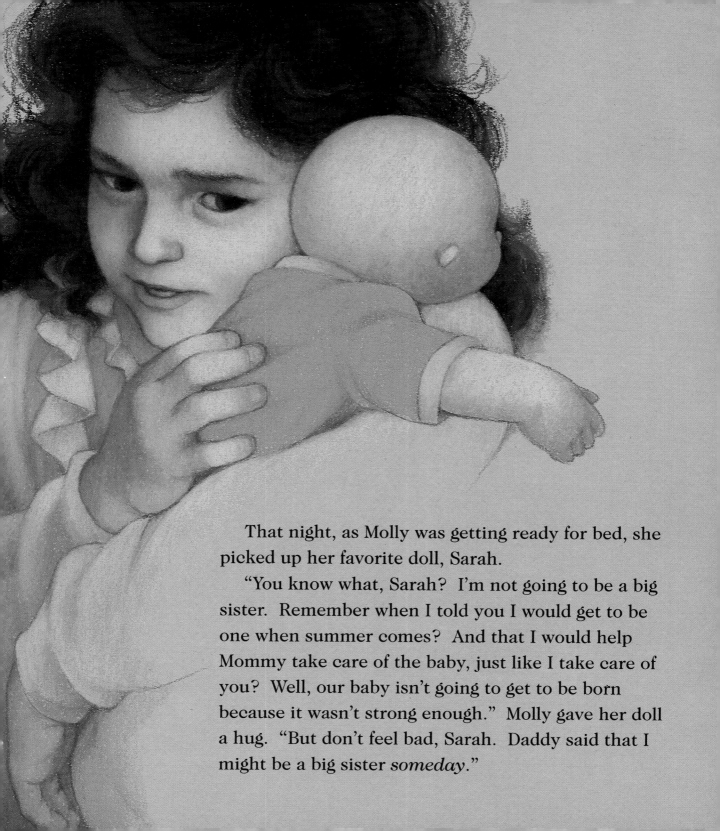

That night, as Molly was getting ready for bed, she picked up her favorite doll, Sarah.

"You know what, Sarah? I'm not going to be a big sister. Remember when I told you I would get to be one when summer comes? And that I would help Mommy take care of the baby, just like I take care of you? Well, our baby isn't going to get to be born because it wasn't strong enough." Molly gave her doll a hug. "But don't feel bad, Sarah. Daddy said that I might be a big sister *someday*."

The next morning, Molly and her grandma took a
walk in the park. They stopped under a tall maple
tree whose branches were all bare because it was
winter. Molly's grandmother reminded her that last
spring, when the tree was full of leaves and birds,
they had seen a robin's nest on a big, sturdy branch.

"Remember when we saw the robin sitting on her eggs? And we found one egg on the ground, that hadn't hatched?"

Molly nodded.

"Well, not every robin's egg becomes a baby robin. Babies don't always get to be born. This happens with people and with all living things. That's why when a baby does get born, it's so special and wonderful. I remember the day you were born, Molly. How happy we all were!"

Molly smiled. "I'm glad I got to be born."

"And so am I," said her grandmother, giving her a squeeze.

Molly and her grandma walked to the end of the park. "Mommy and Daddy feel sad about our baby," Molly said after a while.

"Yes, I know. And how do you feel?"

"Sad, I guess," Molly said.

Grandma nodded. "It's a sad time for all of us." She bent down and looked into Molly's eyes. "Sometimes sad things happen and we don't understand why. All we can do is just feel whatever way we are feeling and try to help each other feel better. What do you think would make you feel better, Molly?"

Molly thought for a moment,
for she wasn't really sure.

"How would you like it if we
spent some extra time
together—just the two of us?
We could bake oatmeal
cookies," Grandma suggested.

"Oh, yes," Molly said.
"And maybe we could do
something to help Mommy
feel better, too. I heard
her crying this morning."

"I think a hug and a kiss
from you would be a real
comfort to her," Grandma said.

"I could do that," said Molly,
"and give her an *extra* big hug."

"I have another idea," said her grandmother. "Why don't you and I walk to the plant store and get a special plant for Mommy?"

"Mommy likes roses," Molly said. "Pink roses are her favorite."

"Yes, they are," her grandmother agreed. "Let's see if we can order a little rosebush that we can plant in the spring."

And that's just what they did. When
spring came, when the ground was soft
and warm, Molly and her parents
planted the bush in their
favorite part of the garden.

As the days became filled with sun and warmth, they watched it sprout leaves, then buds, and finally, flowers. Once in a while, Molly noticed a bud that hadn't bloomed, and it made her a little sad. But almost all of the roses did bloom. And the rosebush would bloom again, every summer.

Dr. Janice Cohn is a psychotherapist who has specialized for the past twenty years in helping children and adults cope with grief and loss. She is the author of I Had a Friend Named Peter: Talking to Children About the Death of a Friend *and* Why Did It Happen? Helping Children Cope in a Violent World. *She practices in Montclair, New Jersey, and New York City.*

I'm indebted to the following people: my editor, Kathy Tucker, who has the ability to know just what I want to say and how to help me say it; Dr. Jack Clemente, whose clinical knowledge (and poetic soul) enriched the manuscript; Sue Zelov, whose attunement to the cycles of nature provided valuable help with the book's imagery; Dr. Rona Kurtz, whose insight, suggestions, and clinical talents were critical; Heide Lange, of Sandford J. Greenberger Associates, whose suggestions and criticism regarding the original manuscript helped make the book a reality; and Lynn Smilow, whose help, encouragement, and enthusiasm regarding the initial idea for this project have been much appreciated. J.C.

Library of Congress Cataloging-in-Publication Data

Cohn, Janice.
  Molly's rosebush / Janice Cohn; illustrated by Gail Owens.
     p.   cm.
  Summary: When the new baby they've been expecting
isn't strong enough to be born, Molly and her family find
different ways to express their feelings and comfort each other.
  ISBN 0-8075-5213-5
  (I. Babies—Fiction. 2. Death—Fiction. 3. Grief—Fiction.)
I. Owens, Gail, ill. II. Title.
PZ7.C665Mo 1994
(E)—dc20   93-50612
                                                   CIP
                                                   AC

Calligraphy by Robert Borja.
Illustrations are done in pastel.